Training in Kingdom

Robert Hall

contents

CHAPTER 1

1 815 in London

Lavinia watched him flash her a brazen grin, sending a thrill rushing through her body. Madam, what brings you to the stables? He was wearing a bordeaux silk robe, and she saw his smoky eyes as they moved across her body.

"Haythorne, I wanted to see how our horses were doing."

The man grinned broadly in amusement. Your horses are in good hands, I can promise you, Madam.

He was honoured by Lavinia's cheeky smirk. She drew nearer to him. I didn't come for just that, though. Lavinia gave him a mouth-to-mouth kiss.

"Please, Madam. I will be fired if anyone discovers us.

A finger of silence was placed on his lips by Lavinia. She persisted in insisting defiantly on being kissed. The groom eventually gave in to the persistent kisses. His tough muscles were the target of Lavinia's finger-rubbing. She said softly into his ear, "I can tell you've done the labour of a true guy. And kindly, let's end the Madams now. It reminds me of my mother-in-law. After all, I'm just five and twenty. She took a quick look at his protruding member. She let out a chuckle of amusement. "I think you're enjoying it," she said.

To Lavinia's strokes, Stuart Haythorne gave in. Lavinia kissed him back, and they both fell to the ground. His top was covered by Lavinia. I should not be with the Marchioness of Coltfield, please.

"Sssh," she reassured. She touched his painful arousal with her hand. She asked as she touched his organ, "Is this so terrible?

"No, not at all bad." As the lovely feelings surrounded him, he closed his eyes. "But Marchioness, why me? The Marquess of Coltfield was the man you were married to.

A high-pitched screech surprised them both before she had a chance to respond. Lavinia gently turned her head so she could identify the voice's owner. When she realised who had made the loud yell, her heart began to race. She jumped up in a hurry. You must be wondering what occurred, Lady Howlington. A pretty straightforward explanation exists. I stumbled while coming here to check on our horses. Ladies shouldn't hang out in the stables.

Quickly rising, the groom groomed himself. When I attempted to save the Marchioness from falling, my foot tripped over some hay.

"And you simply fell to the ground together. I suppose that's a totally valid explanation. Her gaze flitted back and forth between Lavinia and the groom. "I came out here to get some fresh air. Sorry for the screech. I suppose I was right when I assumed there had been some type of accident.

You were quite correct, Lavinia remarked. "Everything was just a coincidence,"

She responded, "Of course," and she grinned a little. "I'm sure that's exactly what occurred.She took a peek at the floor. As soon as everything is OK, I'll go back to the house, she murmured, looking up. You ought to be returning, Lady Coltfield. At the elegant dinner party, dessert is ready to be served. Lady Howlington quickly made a U-turn and headed home.

As she made her way back to the home, Lavinia followed her with her eyes. The groom enquired, "Do you think she'll talk?"

Lavinia chuckled mockingly. "No, I don't think she'll talk, but I'm sure she will talk," I said.

"Lady Coltfield, you are an extremely egotistical being."

"How impolite. You will be let go, I promise.

You won't need to worry. I'll undoubtedly lose my job once word spreads about what she just witnessed. What are you waiting for, then? Visit again for dessert. Your just rewards, in my opinion.

And confront the tumult of the tonnes?

"You ought to have considered that before you tempted me," I said.

"Haythorne, you're totally wrong about that. I fell over some hay. That was the only interaction we had. The two of us would benefit if you kept it in mind.

"Perhaps you are right, my Lady, but if I'm right about the ladies of the tonne, we won't be believed."

"Of course, you are probably right. I've always felt unique compared to the other women.

"Different? You, my lady, epitomise all that is wrong with high bred ladies.

Haythorne asked, "And what is that?"

"You stated as much. You all require a true man. The only thing those Lords, Earls, and Dukes are capable of is eating with the correct utensils. However, they are not proficient in using their own utensils, if you understand what I mean, which I believe you do.

Stuart's insightful observations made Lavinia chuckle uncontrollably. "Haythorne, I can't enter that home again. Are you willing to drive my carriage to my home?

And incur the wrath of both my employer and your future mother-in-law.

"Please be sympathetic. I already have a tonne of scorn.

"My Lady, you can't really blame them. After all, you've been a real vixen since your husband passed away two years ago.

You don't understand what these past two years have meant to me, Haythorne. For the past two years, I have felt nearly free.

Just wishing... As a dejected expression passed her face, she ceased speaking. Haythorne, won't you think twice?

"My Lady, I'm sorry. You will be fighting the Philistines by yourself. Already, my situation is precarious. I can't take the chance, Marchioness.

Lavinia gave a shrug. Then I'll make the short walk back to my house.

"A lady walking down the street alone at this hour of the night won't look proper."

I'm not proper, whoever stated that. This vixen is leaving for a nighttime stroll. I'll miss you, Haythorne, and best of luck. She emerged from the stables and turned to look at the Mayfair townhouse her mother-in-law called home as she approached the front of the building. She was aware that if she returned to that home, she would be punished. Her meeting with the groom was already a matter of discussion.

Lavinia calculated that the distance to her Mayfair townhouse would take her around twenty minutes to walk. She inhaled deeply before setting off on her return trip to her house. She felt strangely liberated as she walked by the Palladian-style townhouses, many of which belonged to Earls and Dukes. It appeared as though her spirit had been set free upon leaving the carriage. A male voice shouting "freedom" jolted her out of her thoughts.She whirled around to look at the source of the baritone voice. A hackney carriage owned by Raven stopped in the street. Lavinia's topaz eyes were met by a set of brandy eyes as she experienced an electric charge throughout her body.

CHapter 2

Lavinia remained motionless on the pavement while the whisky eyes kept her spellbound. From the midnight carriage came a man. Instead of the other passenger's bronze eyes, this one had aqua eyes. Do you need any assistance, Miss?

Lavinia responded, "No, I'm OK.

"I detest seeing a woman alone herself on the streets. You're more than welcome to ride in the hackney. I'll be responsible for covering the charge.

That was really thoughtful of you, sir.Lavinia caught another sight of the cognac eyes and felt inclined to accept the offer. The compassionate man helped her into the carriage after she provided the jarvey her address. Lavinia discovered herself seated across from the person with the whisky eyes. Those eyes snatched her attention, and he slowly let go of her. She observed their eyes steadily lowering their focus till they found her prodigious cleavage. Lavinia's eyes also began to avert until they finally fixed on a stunning sight. The handcuffs that bound a hairy wrist to a bar on the coach door held her eyes captive.

The man watched where Lavina's attention had focused. "My Lady, I see you have located my handcuffs."

The other passenger remarked, "My Lady, don't be alarmed." "I'm Charley, a night watchman of sorts. There is perfect control over this animal. I'm dragging him towards the goal.

The question "What did he do?" Lavinia asked.

"He punched one of the Dukes in the face."

Lavinia struggled to control her giggle. "Sir, what did this Duke do to aggravate you?"

He was one of those renegade Dukes who frequently visited the Cock and Bull pub.

And I'm assuming you visit the Cock and Bull Tavern as well?

"I should be there," I said. I understand my position in society. I believe we should all remain in our respective spaces, my Lady. Anyway, to continue my narrative, I struck this Duke in the face since he showed interest in my girlfriend.

"Well, I guess he deserved it."

The question is, "Do I have a champion, my Lady?"

"Why do you call me my Lady so much? How do you know I'm deserving of the greeting?

Once more, Lavinia's body was being examined by those whisky eyes. "Those hands have never worked for a single day. And without a doubt, you must have the means to acquire pricey outfits.The man paused before continuing. There is always another explanation, of course.

"Which one is?"

That you are a courtesan who may have quarrelled with your patron. That would account for your being in the street.

"Don't be impertinent," the Charley advised. "My Lady, I do apologise for this lout. You are clearly a well-bred person.

I am the Marchioness of Coltfield, Lavinia drew up her shoulders and said with a scornful twist of her head.

The prisoner was struck in the arm by Charley. "Be respectful, Manville. A Marchioness is here, and you are in her presence.

Manville mockedly bowed his head. "Please accept my apology, Lady, I should have known. I commit to using good manners going forward.

The head of Charley was bowed. "Marchioness, it is a pleasure to travel in this carriage with you. I'm sorry for the situation.

As Lavinia gracefully took the compliments, her head dipped. She slowly cocked her head towards Manville. She was intrigued by more than just his acute jawline and dark brown hair. She soaked in the unadulterated, almost primordial atmosphere that was around him. They both held each other's sight as his judging eyes fixed her with an obnoxious look. Lavinia had to avert her own scrutinising eyes since the glare was so intense.

Manville was the one who finally spoke. "I recognise the Marchioness of Coltfield. That name is one I've heard before.

"Manville, don't worry us with your babbling. A man like you would never learn about the Marchioness of Coltfield anywhere on earth, right?

I believe I heard your name mentioned a couple times at the Cock and Bull Tavern.

And what about my name have you heard?

"My Lady, I'd prefer not to say."

If you're honest, I won't hold anything against you.

"Alluring, spirited, and...."

Please go ahead, Lavinia pleaded.

"My Lady, are you certain?" Manville was curious. Lavinia nodded, and Manville replied, "a trollop."

"Manville," Charley remarked angrily, "the Marchioness would never patronise a tavern in that shady area of town. Either you are misinformed or you are displaying terrible breeding.

Surely I'm wrong, Marchioness. You are undoubtedly a beautiful and well-bred woman. Nothing being mentioned could possibly be true, according to Manville.

Lavinia didn't object in any way. She actually recalled spending a lot of nights at the Cock and Bull pub. There were many flirtations with lower-class men, some of which resulted in greater fulfilment.

"My Lady, Manville won't bother you any more. You probably deal with well-bred folks more often than this loose in the haft.

Lavinia again tried to catch Manville's eye. As a small grin crossed his face, she could see the haughtiness in those whisky eyes. "My Lady, I apologise. Charley is correct. I do have a shaky moral code. It appeared as though he was aware of her emotions. She loved the idea of being a loose in the haft instead of being afraid of it. At least he was unable to observe how her private area trembled in response to the statement.

The carriage finally came to a stop on the roadway. The Charley said, "We must have arrived at your house, my Lady."

Manville took one look at the house. The gleaming white Mayfair townhouse was ideal for the stunning Marchioness of Coltfield. Your hubby must be looking forward to seeing you.

The Marquess of Coltfield, my spouse, passed away two years ago.

Manville said, "My sympathies.

Likewise, mine, my lady. I'll now get out of the way and assist you in leaving the carriage, said Charley.

A sudden grief overcame Lavinia, and she cast a glance at the silent, melancholy Manville. Then she got out of the carriage.

After saying her thanks to Charley, she made her way to her front door. She watched as the carriage moved down the street. As she made her way inside her house, she pondered what would happen to Manville.

Chapter 3

There was silence throughout the house. Lavinia was vividly conscious of how alone she was after the servants had gone to bed. She removed her shoes before entering the living room. She sat down on her red, silk chaise lounge and splayed out. She could only see glimpses of the man she had just met when she closed her eyes. His powerful jaw, bulky arms, eyes, voice, and spirit encircled her completely.

Lavinia pulled the bell. Her maid soon made her way into the drawing room. She waited for her instructions while standing at attention with her head lowered. Please bring me some sherry, Dorothy.

I agree, Madam. She went out to perform her tasks. She delivered a decanter of sherry for her mistress when she entered the drawing room. While waiting for more orders, she poured herself a drink. "Please sit down, Dorothy.Lavinia drank some sherry after Dorothy settled on the red silk chair. "I'm having trouble."

"Madam, I'm sorry to hear that."

I'm sure I made quite a scandal tonight.

I agree, Madam.

"I understand that you're uncomfortable, but the truth is that I really need to talk to someone," Dorothy said. I'm trying to convey that it's okay to express your true feelings to me. Your employment won't be in danger.

I agree, Madam.

"Since I know the servants would discuss what happened, I might as well tell you what happened. I was discovered by Lady Howlington atop the dowager Lady Coltfield's groom.

Lavinia was aware of Dorothy's expression of worry. Did Lady Coltfield discuss it with you?

"No, I got out of the dinner party before she could."

The question, "Where was your groom?"

As soon as I entered the dinner gathering, I let him know he could leave. The Coltfield's groom typically returns to my house in my carriage, then either walks or takes a hackney. Sometimes, Dorothy, I do feel bad for my staff. Whenever I can, I give them a break.

"Madam, you have shown the servants a lot of kindness. Much more kind than. Dorothy's voice became halting.

Than the Marquess of Coltfield, my dearly gone husband? Dorothy apologetically nodded. "Don't worry, Dorothy. My husband treated me with the same strictness as he did the servants. He insisted on perfect decorum at all times. Including the bedroom.

Lavinia noticed Dorothy's blushing face. "Madam, perhaps I shouldn't hear from you anymore."

"Anyway, he's in my past. Now that I've been a widow for two years, it's time for me to be married once more.

If I may be so bold, Madam, do you have a suitor?

"Yes, Dorothy, you might be so brave. No, I don't currently have any suitors. As visions of Manville began to creep into Lavinia's mind, she grew silent.

"Perhaps dowager Lady Coltfield can be of assistance. She is familiar with every single ton's eligible bachelor.

"Yes, that's what she does." Lavinia gulped down more sherry in a flash. "She could find me some fop just like her son," I remarked. Lavinia restrained herself from expressing to her maid her darkest desires. Not for a different aristocrat, though. She wanted to be in the embrace of the melancholy man she had just met in the raven carriage. She'll never see him again. A girl as attractive as you must have attracted suitors, right Dorothy? Lavinia made a light probe.

I've had a couple.

Have they served as footmen, groomsmen, or butlers, possibly?

"Yes, mainly."

It must have been wonderful.

"I'm not sure, Madam. I occasionally have dreams where I'm being held by a duke. resembles Cinderella in several ways. Stupid, huh?"

Not at bit foolish, Dorothy.There was a knock at the door, and Lavinia grinned at her maid.

The footman showed there by the door after Lavinia bid to enter. Lord and Lady Coltfield have come to see you, Madam.

I anticipated this situation, but not at this hour of the night.

The late husband's parents arrived at the door before the footman had a chance to respond. After setting her sherry glass down, Lavinia got up from her chair. "Lord and Lady Coltfield, please come in."

When Lady Coltfield came in, she immediately expressed displeasure when she saw Dorothy seated in the chair. Dorothy stood up and curtsied quickly. She bobbed her head before leaving the room. Do your staff members always join you for a drink, Lavinia?

"Only if I want them to. Please take a seat.

I'm not going to hold back with you, Lavinia. This evening, you tarnished the Coltfield name.

I am aware that I am not the bride you had dreamed your son would wed.

You're not, I say.

Lord Coltfield made a statement. Margaret, perhaps you might be a little kinder.

It's time for hard honesty, I'm afraid. The reputation of our family depends on it. As Lady Coltfield spoke, Lavinia poured herself another glass of sherry and sat back in her chair. "I'm not going to let you tarnish the Coltfield name. Next month, my granddaughter will begin her first season.

"I have no doubt she'll have great success finding a decent husband."

Nothing, Lady Coltfield said, "is guaranteed." "That's why it's so crucial that you pick the right husband in the coming thirty days."

Lavinia lowered her glass. "I'm assuming you're aware of the provision in my deceased husband's will."

"Lavinia, I most definitely do know. The condition specifies that in order to keep receiving your allowance, you must be married within two years. I am also aware of the clause that demands my consent before you choose a husband, or else your allowance will be donated to the charity of your choice.

"Lady Coltfield, I am as interested in finding a husband as you are in my doing so."

You're there, Lavinia. You're known to frequent dive bars till the wee hours of the morning.

Many people talk about your lustful behaviour.

"Lady Coltfield, you must know of the propensity among some married men of the tonne," she said.

Lord Coltfield decided to pour himself a glass of sherry. He sipped the sherry and then reclined in the chair. I never told you this, but I really do like you, Lavinia.

I do recall, Lord Coltfield, that you welcomed me into your family.

"I must admit, I had some reservations about my son getting married to you. Your fair skin and dark hair really made for a seductive combination, in my opinion. Your skeletal structure is also unquestionably patrician enough. I could see why my kid was attracted to you. However, I was concerned by something about you.

Lavinia was observed by Lord Coltfiled to determine her reaction. He kept talking. "Lavinia, you have fire within of you. I was aware that you could never be content to resemble the other ladies of the tavern. Lord Coltfield gulped down more sherry. I was aware of your contempt for aristocratic customs, and you are correct that women face discrimination in our society. However, you cannot alter the current situation. You must decide what to do. You have to find a good husband or you'll lose your allowance.

"I value your candour, Lord Cotlfield. I want to be honest right now.

Lord Coltfield asked politely.

I questioned if Lady Coltfield would be completely impartial if she accepted my choice of husband.

Lady Coltfield gave her daughter-in-law a stern look. Are you going to permit her to address me in such a manner?

"Don't worry, Margaret. Her husband informed her that her doubt was perfectly normal. Would you care to respond?

"My family's reputation is really important to me. To stop the rumours and scandals, I would love to see you as a respectable member of society. At the same time, I won't let you wed a scoundrel or a rascal. I prefer that the funds be donated to a deserving cause. Lavinia, you have my word that I will treat you fairly since I am a Christian.

"Thank you for that, Lady Coltfield. I'll try my hardest to find a good husband.

Then, Lavinia, that is all we can ask for. Standing, Lord Coltfield. "And with that, we'll say goodbye. Lavinia, I'm sure you'll have a good night's rest tonight.

Lavina stood up. Lord and Lady Coltfield, thank you. Travel safely home.

Lavinia poured herself one last sherry glass. She ascended the staircase to her bedroom. In her personal sanctuary, she felt secure. She took off her clothes in order to avoid upsetting her maid once more. She closed her eyes as she sat down on the four-poster bed. She sat back in a warm contentment as Manville's primitive face crept into her thoughts.

CHAPTER 4

Lavinia wore a sky-blue muslin dress as she took a morning stroll through her gardens. She hoped that it would help settle her nerves. After she finished gazing at the delicate roses, she entered her drawing room. There was a side buffet of breakfast foods ready for the arrival of her solicitor. She knew that the news he brought was of vital importance to her future. There was no way she could fend off reality anymore.

The footman announced his arrival. "Good morning, Lady Coltfield," the solicitor said, as he entered the drawing room.

"Good morning, Mr. Johnstone. Please help yourself to some breakfast, Mr. Johnstone. The plum cake is particularly delicious."

"Thank you," the portly solicitor replied. He helped himself to a healthy slice of plum cake and then sat down "Lady Coltfield, I asked for this appointment to discuss your late husband's will."

"Please begin."

"As you know, your husband's will has a provision which stated that you are to find a husband within two years of his death. If you succeed, then your allowance will continue. If you do not succeed, then the allowance will be donated to a charity of your choice." After another bite of the cake, he asked, "Have you succeeded in finding a husband, Lady Coltfield?"

"Not as yet."

"It is my duty to remind you that you have thirty days left in which to do so. I don't wish to pry, but is there some reason as to why you haven't succeeded as of yet?"

"I simply don't wish to marry."

"Lady Coltfield, I feel it is my duty to remind you that it is in your best interests to abide by your husband's wishes. Not only will your allowance continue, but your husband will inherit Lord Coltfield's considerable properties." He looked kindly at Lavinia. "Certainly, a woman of your beauty should have no trouble finding a husband."

"One would think that, I suppose. However, I fear I am most unmarriageable."

"Because of your trysts with unsavory sorts of men?" He paused, then continued. "I'm sorry for being so blunt, but there is no other way to be at this moment. Your inheritance depends on it. "

"I'm afraid the only man who will marry me is a desperate rake, a fortune hunter, or...." Lavinia paused, as she pondered another possibility.

"Go on," he prodded.

"Or a man desperate for his freedom."

"If you're talking about a prisoner, he will never get the approval of the dowager Lady Coltfield."

"Money has always been known to buy a man's freedom, hasn't it?"

"I suppose at times, it has. It depends what the offense is."

Mr. Johnstone studied his client, and then spoke. "Lady Coltfield, may I remind you that the Marquess's mother will be looking for certain qualities. She's looking for a refinement and elegance that won't be found in a common prisoner."

"Yes, you're right, of course. I'd never even consider introducing a criminal to dowager Lady Coltfield."

"I must inform you that the dowager Lady Coltfield has set a date for her to meet your chosen husband. She will arrange for a dinner party where you can introduce your future husband to the haute monde."

"Another dinner party? I don't know if I can survive one."

"You must survive, Lady Coltfield. Your future depends on it. It's not pleasant for a woman who is without financial support. You might even be forced to seek employment."

"What kind of work could I possibly do?"

"You could work in a shop, you could be a governess, or......"

"Or what?"

He took a deep breath and plunged forward. "You could be a lady's maid."

"Mr.Johnstone if you are trying to scare me, you have been successful."

"Lady Coltfield, I'm not trying to scare you. I'm just trying to get you to accept the seriousness of your situation."

"You have certainly done that. You can rest assured that I will try very hard to bring a suitable husband to Lady Coltfield."

He nodded. "Then I will take my leave, Lady Coltfield. " He bowed and then departed from the room.

Lavinia leaned back in her chair. She tried to digest all that Mr. Johnstone had just told her. It was either marriage to another man like her late husband, or she could plunge forward with her idea. She rang the bell pull. When Dorothy appeared, she said, "Please tell the groom I will have need for my coach. And bring my pelisse."

"Yes, Madam." Dorothy went off to attend to her duties. She returned with her mistresses' pelisse.

As she helped Lavinia into the blue silk overcoat, she said, "The groom is waiting with your coach, Madam. "

She walked with Dorothy to the front door, and then stepped forward into the street. She told the groom what her destination was. Unperturbed by the alarm on her groom's face, she stepped into her carriage. As the carriage plodded down the streets, her heart pounded in anticipation. Soon, she would be reunited with the dark man she had met in a raven carriage.

CHAPTER 5

Heath Manville wiped the sweat off his brow. The thought of another night's sleep on the straw mattress the prison supplied filled him with disgust. "All this trouble just for punching a Duke," he said aloud.

"Is that all you did?" a fellow cell mate replied. "I pick pocketed some Lords, that's why I'm here. That seems more worthy than your petty crime."

"How long have you been here?" Heath inquired.

"It's been two months now. I'm still waiting for my trial." The fellow prisoner lifted himself off the straw floor. "Let me introduce myself. I'm Barnaby Rowles."

"Heath Manville. Two months of this hell? How do you manage?"

"I had some money to pay for some basic needs, and it's helped. I've just about run out, though. How are you fixed for money?"

"Your skills would be wasted on me, lad. There's nothing in my pockets."

"Then you'll be short of food, I can tell you."

Heath looked around at his fellow prisoners. There were nine other men in the cell with him. Heath wondered whether he'd survive the dreary conditions.

There wasn't any further time for Heath to ponder his misfortune. A loud command came forth. "Manville, get you arse front and center."

Heath did as he was told. The cell door opened and a burly man pushed him forward, and out of the cell door. "You've got a visitor, and a real beauty at that. A lady like herself doesn't belong in this squalor. You'll see her upstairs." Heath was shoved upstairs into the more hospitable conditions of the upper chambers. A guard escorted him into a room with windows. "The prisoner, Heath Manville."

Lavinia stood before Heath in all her intoxicating beauty. He bowed deeply when he saw who his visitor was. "Lady Coltfield, I am humbled by your visit."

A feeling of warmth stole over Lavinia's body as she stared at the prisoner. "I was thinking about your predicament and I wanted to help."

"How kind of you, Lady Coltfield. But why would you want to help a man you barely know?"

"I thought that it was rather silly to bring you to jail for punching a Duke."

"And that is the only reason you are here?"Heath inquired-with a penetrating stare.

"There is something else. I have come to you with a proposition." Lavinia hoped she could disguise the shiver which coursed through her.

"Continue."

"I need to find a husband within thirty days."

"And how do I fit in? "

"I need you to be my husband."

"Lady Coltfield, surely a woman as beautiful as yourself can have your pick of men. Why a man you barely know, and a prisoner, at that?"

"I am a scandalized woman."

"And what will be the terms of this arrangement, if I choose to accept?"

"After a period of training, you will be presented to my late husband's mother, the dowager Lady Coltfield. If you are acceptable to her, the marriage ceremony will take place."

"And if I am unacceptable? Then what will happen to me?"

"I've never really thought about that. I suppose you will be free to go your own way."

"That was a very interesting phrase, Lady Coltfield. If I am rejected by the dowager Lady Coltfield, I will be free. "Lavinia assessed Heath carefully. She realized that she had more in common with her intended husband than she thought. "And if I am accepted, what will be the terms of our marriage?"

"You will have all customary rights accorded to husbands. "

"All customary rights." He scanned her body. "Let us clarify what that means. Are we talking about property or conjugal rights?"

Lavinia pondered this. She hadn't really thought about it. "I suppose we will have to see what develops. If I decide to share my body with you, then you shall have your conjugal rights."

"My Lady, I can only accept your offer on one condition. Conjugal rights will only happen if, and when, I decide it shall happen."

"I must say you're impertinent for a man in your position. I would think you would want your freedom under any circum stances."."

"I see my choice as deciding between the lesser of the two evils. Imprisonment in this hell hole of a prison, or imprisonment in more desirable surroundings."

"So, what will your decision be, Manville?"

Heath dwelled upon his choices. As he did so, he raked his eyes over Lavinia. Suddenly, the guard spurted out, "Don't be foolish, man. Take this beautiful lady's offer, or your food supply will be cut short, I can assure you."

"You are right. I haven't the resources to pay for my present grand circumstances. Marchioness Coltfield, I accept your offer."

Lavinia said brusquely, "Fine. Then I will make the final arrangement with the governor."

The guard said, "Marchioness, I will bring the prisoner to you when he is formally released."

"I will be waiting in my coach."

Heath bowed deeply. "Until we meet again. Marchioness."

Lavinia watched as Heath was escorted out of the room by the guard. The guard brought him to the bowels of the goal again. He shoved him back into the dark and dank cell. "On your feet, gentlemen. You are in the presence of a Marquess."

None of the prisoners bothered to get up. "What's all this nonsense about being a Marquess," Barnaby asked. "You don't look like you have an aristocratic bone in your body."

"How true," Heath concurred. "I am about as far from being an aristocrat as it comes."

"Manville," the guard snapped, "wait here until we come for you."

"Heath, are you getting your freedom?" Barnaby asked.

"That depends on how you view things, I suppose," Heath answered.

"Anything is better than this living hell. How did you get out?"

"By accepting a proposal of marriage from a vixen."

"That's nothing to worry about, Heath. Just let her know who the master is."

"I intend to," Heath replied. And as he waited for his freedom, he repeated, "I intend to."

Chapter 6

Lavinia waited outside the goal for the arrival of Heath Manville. She was aware that her bonnet and spencer were out of place in this part of London. Surely, there were no Dukes or Earls here. Many a loose fish passed her by, and some had rather coarse comments. However, she chose to remain on the street so Heath Manville would remember why he got his freedom.

A large, burly man approached Lavinia. "What do we have here? "The man nodded his approval. "A diamond of the first order," he pronounced. "And banged up to the mark."

"I'm not interested if you think I'm dressed up in high fashion."

He inched in closer to Lavinia. "I'll decide what's my business, my Lady."

"I am asking you to back away. You are too close to me."

"Am I now?" came the cockney accent. He inched in further to Lavinia, and pulled her to his body. Lavinia fought desperately to push him off of her. Just as she gave a forceful thrust, the door of the goal opened.

Heath immediately grabbed the man off of Lavinia. He lifted him up by his collar. "Is there a problem, man?"

"No, not at all, sir. I was just admiring the beautiful lady, that's all."

Heath let the man down. "Be off with you then. You've finished your business here."

"Yes sir, I'll be off now." He ran as fast as he could down the street.

"Are you alright, Marchioness?" Heath inquired.

"Yes, I'm fine. Thank you, Heath."

Heath bowed deeply. "My captors have delivered me to you, my Lady. I await your further direction."

"We're going to my country seat. I've already sent my staff there."

"A country home. I've always loved the country."

They walked to the carriage. The groom held the door open for Lavinia and Heath. "After you, my Lady." Heath bowed as Lavinia entered the carriage. He settled into the opposite seat from Lavinia. The carriage started its journey to Lavinia's country seat. "Once again, we find ourselves in a carriage. That is how we first met."

Lavinia brushed aside Heath's comment with a curt, "Yes, I do recall that. Now, let's discuss the particulars of our arrangement."

"Of course, my Lady."

"I think we should introduce you as Sir Heath. You are a distant relative of my late husband."

"That would make sense. Where will I sleep?"

"There's a guest cottage. You'll sleep there," Lavinia pronounced.

"As you wish, my Lady. For now, anyway."

Lavinia didn't say anything. "You might as well start calling me Lavinia in private."

"That is very kind of you, Lavinia. Lavinia has such a lovely sound to it."

"Now, we have to talk about your clothing. I will l arrange for a haberdasher to come to the home. You have to start looking the part of a knight."

"Is that what I am now?"

"It's what you are to become. "

"And what else about me will change?"

"Almost everything, I imagine."

"Almost everything. What is the part you would like to preserve, Lavinia?" Lavinia could feel her cheeks growing warm. "Never mind, Lavinia. There's time enough to find out."

"I can see we will have to change your crude way of speaking."

"You have a big challenge in front of you, Lavinia."

"I've never been afraid of a challenge, Heath."

"Nor have I, Lavinia."

"That is good, because I think there's a lot of work to be done before you are turned into a Marquess."

"Perhaps it can't be done."

"If you want to partake of the rewards waiting for you, then you had better do it."

"Rewards," Heath repeated. "You know, we never did settle the matter about my conjugal rights."

"A gentleman would never bring that up."

"Perhaps, but isn't that why I'm sitting here? Because I'm not like the men you are accustomed to meeting in the haute monde?"

"Heath, you are just like any other man to me."

"We shall see. Heath looked intently at Lavinia. "Will there be any children afoot?"

"No, my marriage produced no children."

"May I be so bold as to inquire why not?"

"My husband and I had sparse conjugal encounters. "

"Most men would enjoy your womanly charms."

"My husband found me rather aggressive."

"He couldn't handle you."

"He sought his fulfilment elsewhere."

"And you were content to live a life of luxury, and remain with a man who couldn't satisfy your appetites." Heath said it more as a pronouncement and not a question. Lavinia locked eyes with Heath and then looked away. She fought to hold back tears but they trickled down her cheeks. She was surprised when she felt Heath's hand touch her cheek. "Why are there tears in your eyes, Lavinia?"

"I'm not sure," she answered. That wasn't entirely true. Lavinia wasn't ready to tell a near stranger about all the empty nights of the soul she had endured while married to her husband. "Divorce was never an option."

"No, of course not," Heath agreed. "Still, it kills the spirit when there is no love in a marriage."

Lavinia's hand caressed the male hand that was still lay upon her cheek. Her lips pursed as she held Heath's gaze. "I shouldn't be bothering you with my troubles, Heath. It's not appropriate."

Heath rose from his seat and crossed over to sit beside Lavinia. "Let me decide what is appropriate, Lavinia." Lavinia didn't' say anything as Heath pulled her closer to him. Lavinia's head dropped onto his shoulder. He gently patted her head.

She raised her head a bit. "Heath, you don't have to...."

Heath silenced her with a tender finger placed on her lips. "Sssh, my Lady, it's time for you to rest now."

Lavinia didn't object. She put her head back on Heath's shoulder, as the carriage continued its journey to the country home they would now share.

CHAPTER 7

Heath watched from his window as the carriage made its way up the winding path to the palatial house. The coachman had opened the coach door. Heath gently nudged Lavinia. She had fallen asleep on Heath's shoulder. "My lady, we have arrived at your palace."

Lavinia half opened her eyes, but remained on Heath's shoulder. Heath noted Lavina's fatigue, and made his decision. He gently scooped Lavinia up into his arms, and descended from the carriage with her. The coachman said, "Be careful with her, sir. The Marchioness has been very good to us."

"You've nothing to worry about", Heath assured him. "He carried her to the entrance of the gleaming white home.

As Heath waited for the door to open, Lavinia slowly opened her eyes. Awareness slowly came to her. "Heath, put me down."

"In a moment, my Lady."

The butler tried to disguise his surprise when he opened the door. "Madam, are you alright?"

"I think so. "

"Madam is fine," Heath reassured. Heath entered the hall. "Please point me to the parlor." Heath found the parlor with his assistance. He deposited Lavinia onto the chaise.

"Why were you carrying me, Heath?"

"You seemed to need the assistance."

"Nonsense. I've always been able to take care of myself."

"No harm meant, my Lady."

"Never mind that for now. We have other matters to take care of." Lavinia surveyed Heath from head to foot. "You might as well sit down." Heath sat opposite her. "It's about time for dinner. We shall see how you eat."

"I assure you I am quite uncouth. I can gobble up a whole hog without coming up for air."

"You probably can, but that simply won't do for a knight, or a future marquess. But, before we undertake the mission, you are in dire need of grooming. I will ask the stable boy to assist in bathing you. After all, he's had a lot of practice."

"Practice, my Lady?"

"He has bathed horses, after all."

"Is that what I am to you? "

"What do you mean?"

"Do you look at me like one of your horses?"

Lavinia let her eyes roam over Heath's body. "Horses do go through a period of training."

"Horses need to be broken, my Lady. I can assure you that I can't be broken. "

Lavinia bent her head to the side, a slight smirk on her face. Without further comment, she pulled the bell rope. The butler entered. "Forbes, please have the cook prepare dinner for two. And, please have the stable boy prepare a bath for Sir Heath."

"Surely you don't mean Sir Heath is to have a bath in the stables?"

"Of course not," Lavinia answered. "Please take Heath to the bathroom to have his bath."

"Very well, Madam. I will show you to the bathroom, Sir Heath.

"And see if you could find something for Sir Heath to wear. I left some items from my husband's wardrobe here "

"Certainly, Madam" .

Heath gave a mock bow before he departed with the butler to take his bath. Lavinia decided to fill the time by taking a stroll to the kitchen. The cook curtsied when she saw her mistress. "Becky, I would like to go over the dinner menu with you." "Of course, Marchioness."

"You'll need to prepare dinner for two. I should like some of our fine game, and some luscious desserts."

"Of course, Madam."

"Thank you, Becky."

Lavinia left the kitchen. She walked up the staircase and headed for her late husband's bedroom. There was an adjoining bathroom there, and that is where Heath was having his bath. As Lavinia observed her husband's male retreat, she imagined Heath's muscled body being bathed. Her heart quickened as she thought about viewing him in his naked state. As she stood in the middle of the room, she could hear the splashing sounds of water. She imagined what body part the stable boy was attending to. Her visions were interrupted by the sudden click of the door. She immediately left the bedroom, but wasn't sure if Heath hadn't caught sight of her.

Lavinia returned to her sitting room. She composed herself on her chaise. She pulled the rope bell for the butler. When he entered, she gave him her instructions. "Please have Sir Heath taken to the dining room when he is properly clothed. I will meet him there for dinner."

"Very well, Madam."

After about twenty minutes had past, Lavinia prepared to go to the dining room. When she entered the dining room, Heath was already there, He rose and bowed. "Marchioness, I am ready for your use."

"The first thing we will have to work on is your table manners, and I imagine that will take a lot of work."

"I will do my best to meet your approval, Marchioness."

The maid entered with the soup. She used a tureen to serve her mistress and her guest. Lavinia watched as Heath loudly slurped soup into his mouth.

"You'll have to learn to stop making sounds when you eat, Sir Heath."

"I apologize, Marchioness. Peasants can be so earthy."

Lavinia put her spoon down. "I can see you're going to be a lot of work, Sir Heath."

"Perhaps I am going to be too much for you to handle, Marchioness."

"I can handle you, I assure you."

"We shall see, Marchioness, we shall see." Heath returned to his soup bowl, and slurped even louder than before,

Lavinia rolled her eyes to heaven. "I've made arrangements for you to reside in the guest cottage."

"You mean I'm not to reside in the stables with the other horses?"

"Enough with this talk, Sir Heath. I insist that you sip that soup quietly."

"I'll slurp as loudly as I want."

"Let me remind you that your future depends on how you please me."

"I can assure you I shall please you, my dear Marchioness."

Lavinia returned to her soup bowl, and hoped that her face didn't reveal the quiver which surged through her private part.

CHAPTER 8

Heath was jarred out of his sleep by a knock on the bedroom door. He rose from the massive mahogany bed and opened the door.

"You needn't have gotten out of bed, Sir. You could have just bid me to enter."

"Shouldn't you be attending to the horses?"

"The Marchioness has sent me to assist you."

"Assist me to do what?"

"I shall be your valet. I shall attend to all your needs."

Heath chuckled. "I hate to pull you away from your duties. I know you have horses to attend to I really won't be needing your services."

"Please, Sir Heath. The Marchioness is insistent. It's my job, I do believe you'd understand." The lad looked down at the ground.

"Don't be frightened. I know I'm not very convincing as a knight. How did you figure it all out?"

"You seem like so much more of a man than the fops and dandies who parade around town."

Heath laughed heartily. "So, I wasn't very convincing as a knight." Heath's laughter subsided, as he had his next thought. "The question is, then how am I going to...." But he stopped himself. "Now then, come in, and let me help you keep your employment. "

"Thank you, Sir."

"I'm new to this. What should we do first?"

"The Marchioness said I should have you looking suitable for breakfast in the main house."

"Did she now?"

"Don't worry, Sir. I shall help you. Just sit on that chair and wait for me to attend to you."

Heath settled on the chair as he waited for Luke to attend to his duties. As he waited, he mused on the sudden change in his status. And although the Lady Lavinia grated on him at times, he readily admits that it was better than sending another night at the jail. And o, of course, there was that bewitching beauty he could feast his eyes upon.

Luke came back with the clothes Heath was to wear that day. He laid then out on the bed. "I have your clothes ready, Sir."

"I am to wear all that? Just to have some breakfast?"

"It's the way the proper gentleman dresses, Sir."

Heath got up with a sigh. "Then let us begin."

Luke fetched knee length drawers. Heath just stared at them, and then ft Luke. "You don't mean what I think you mean?"

"I don't understand, Sir."

"You're not going to help me put that on, are you?"

"I assure you I'm very discreet, Sir."

"Luke, please, I am a kindred spirit to you. Surely, you must understand how uncomfortable I am as a man...."

"Say no more, Sir. What is it you'd have me do?"

"Stay outside the room until I call for you."

"Certainly, Sir."

Heath stared incredulously at the amount of clothing a gentleman was required to wear in the morning. By the time he was finished, he had on a snowy white shirt, tan leather breeches, and black waistcoat. "Luke," he called.

"Sir."

"Don't tell me I will be required to wear this every morning?"

"It's how a proper Regency gentleman dresses."

"I am ready, Luke, to be delivered as a proper Regency gentleman to the Marchioness."

Luke bowed, and they both left the bedroom. They descended the mahogany staircase, and as they opened the front door, they were greeted by a bright sun. "Will you need a carriage, Sir?"

"For such a small distance? Manville's are hearty sorts." Heath and his new valet walked to the front entrance of the main house. They were let into the house by the butler, who led Heath to the dining room.

Lavinia waited at the table. "You look quite respectable, Sir Heath. Have you ever seen a proper Regency style breakfast?"

"No, I'm used to eating from a horse's trough."

"I didn't mean to imply anything of the sort."

"Of course not, Marchioness. You're too much of a lady to ever do that."

Lady Lavinia ignored the remark and proceeded to show Heath what the morning buffet consisted of. "The proper thing to do is to take a plate and fill it with anything you'd like."

"I think I can manage that, Lady Lavinia."

Lavinia nodded her approval and then filled her own plate with food. Heath joined her at the dining table. "The most important thing to remember is that you don 't makes slurping sounds when you eat."

"I shall remember that, Lady Lavinia."

Lavinia watched Heath as he ate. "Heath, we have to start talking about your gentlemanly skills."

"I assure you that I possess a great deal of gentlemanly skills."

Lavinia cleared her throat. What we need to discuss is forming you into a Corinthian."

"A what?"

"A Corinthian, a man who can engage in sports. A man who is a master of sword play."

"Does sword play mean fencing?""

"Why yes."

"You seem surprised that I know what sword play means."

"I must admit that I am somewhat surprised. Where did you learn how to fence?"

"Does it matter?'

"I suppose not. "Lavinia took a bite, and then offered, "would you like to show me how you have mastered the sword?"

"Do you have a partner for me?"

"Yes."

"And that is?"

"Me."

"Pardon me, marchioness, but you are a lady."

"I believe that is obvious."

"Ladies don't fence. How did you come to learn how to fence?"

"My father was in the military. He ardently wished for a son, but alas, fate cursed him with a daughter. He was elated when I told him of my desire to fence. Much to my mother's chagrin, he instructed me in the art of fencing."

"Are you challenging me to a duel, Lady Lavinia?"

"I suppose that I am."

"And where will this duel take place?"

"The estate grounds will do."

Heath pinned Lavinia with a long, soul piercing stare. "I see what you want, Marchioness." Heath stood and bowed. "I will meet you on the estate grounds."

"Very well, then. My husband had a dueling outfit you can wear. "

"And what will you wear? Or will you wear anything at all?"

"Of course, I'll wear something. I have a female fencing out-fit."

"Then adieu, Marchioness , until we meet again." Heath took Lavinia's hand and graced it with a soft kiss and then departed the room.

CHAPTER 9

Lavinia waited by the riding ring for Heath to arrive. She was aware of how shocked the ton would be to see a woman clothed in in a long tunic and breeches. She grasped her rapier in her hand as she waited for her opponent.

Heath greeted Lavinia with a deep bow. When he rose, Lavinia could see the bulge in his breeches. "Do you still wish to fence, my lady?"

Lavinia thrust her sword in answer to Heath's question. Heath thrust his blade in response. As the opponents thrusted and parried, Lavinia could feel a delicious excitement consume her body. And when Heath took a step backwards, Lavinia held her head up triumphantly. "Is that the best you can do, Manville?"

"If it is a real battle you want, you will get one, Lady Lavinia." Heath thrust more aggressively until he had his sword poised at Lavinia's throat. They locked eyes. As the rapier was held at Lavinia's throat, his eyes roamed down to Lavinia's breasts. Slowly, his blade drifted down her tunic until it rested beneath her breasts. As Lavinia felt the cold, hard steel of the sword, her insides quivered. She felt her inner part moist and pulsing. She felt strangely filled up in a way that was totally new to her. "You look strangely content for a woman who's just been defeated."

"I still have more fight in me, Manville."

Heath yanked the sword out of Lavinia's hand. He dropped his sword and pulled Lavinia roughly towards him. He kissed her hard on her lips. Lavinia's hands flailed against Heath's shoulders before she surrendered to the sudden burst of passion. Heath pulled his mouth away, as Lavinia's heart beat like a drum. "I believe we are finished with our business for today."

"But," Lavinia was about to say, and she stopped herself. "Then you may go."

Heath let out a hearty laugh. "I'll go when I choose to go."

"You are forgetting that you are here to be trained, Manville. You must meet my standards before you can be introduced as my future husband."

"You can drop your defenses now, Lady Lavinia. I believe that look on your face when I held the sword under your breast spoke more than a thousand protestations."

Lavinia fought hard to keep her face masked. She didn't want Heath to know they way he moved her. The last thing she needed was to be under a man's control. She had been under her husband's control and it had brought her nothing but misery. "If you refuse to go, then I will go. "

"Then I have won another battle, Marchioness."

"You are insufferable," she said.

Heath grabbed her roughly. "It's not to my liking to be trained like a wild horse."

"That is exactly what you agreed to. "

Heath didn't answer. He abruptly turned and walked away from their battle. Lavinia suddenly felt a longing to run after him but she stopped herself. She waited until he was out of sight and then walked back to the house.

As soon as she was in her bedroom she rang for her maid. When Dorothy appeared, she said, "I shall need to wash up before dinner. And, be sure to give word to our guest that he should be here for dinner at 5:00."

"Yes, Madam."

When Dorothy had prepared the bath, Lavinia entered the tub. Dorothy attended to her mistress. "Madam, I know I am being impertinent but you are a little bit more ...." Dorothy suddenly stopped.

"You can finish your thoughts, Dorothy. "

"I was going to say you are a bit filthier, Madam."

"I did have a rather unusual afternoon, Dorothy. I engaged in a fencing match." Dorothy didn't reply. "You can ask me how the duel went, Dorothy." "How did the duel go, Madam?"

"It was unusually stimulating." In fact, even as she lay in the tub, her private parts quivered as she recalled the way Heath's sword lay underneath her breasts. Lavinia looked at Dorothy's face, which had turned a bright red. Lavinia decided to say no more. She closed her eyes and remembered the masterful way Heath dueled with her.

A few hours later, Lavinia was attended to by Dorothy as she prepared for dinner. After she donned a red taffeta dress, she headed for the dining room. Dishes formed a symmetrical and beautiful format in the center of the table. Lavinia poured herself some red wine as she waited for Heath to arrive. After about fifteen minutes, Heath had still not arrived, and Lavinia found herself a bit anxious. As she sipped her white soup, she wondered whether Heath would be there. When 5:30 had arrived, and Heath still wasn't there, she rang for Forbes.

Forbes bowed when he arrived. "Yes, Madam?"

"Forbes, send the stable boy to inform Sir Heath he is late for dinner."

"Yes, Madam."

Lavinia poured herself some more wine as she waited for Heath to arrive. After all, she was offering Heath respectability. He owed her his obedience to her household rules. She heard the knock on the dining room door. She held her head high in victory as she waited for Heath to appear. When she saw who appeared at the door, her heart fell. "Luke, what are you doing here?"

"Madam, Sir Heath has asked me to inform you that he will not be in attendance at dinner tonight."

"And what is the reason for that?"

"He says he is fatigued from the day's activities. He would prefer to dine alone at his residence."

"I see. Very well, that will be all, Luke." When Luke had left the room, Lavinia clutched at the table. An overwhelming feeling of disappointment gripped her. A hot feeling of anger gripped her insides. She felt like it would rip her insides out. Lavinia had lost her appetite and retired to her room. As she sat on the chaise, she felt an overwhelming sense of being alone. Too many nights had passed without her soul being filled up. She knew what she must do. She still donned the red taffeta dress as she headed for Heath's residence.

CHAPTER 10

Lavinia stood before the guest cottage. She weighed her decision in her mind before she rang the door pull. She could proceed with her visit, or she could head back to her lonely room. She decided to ring the door pull.

Luke greeted her with a bow. "Marchioness, please come in."

"Thank you, Luke. "

"Shall I announce your visit to Sir Heath?"

"No, not yet, Luke. I shall like to take a look at the cottage first. I'm thinking of redecorating."

"Very well, Madam."

"Do you know where Sir Heath is?"

"He has retired to his bedroom."

"You may go, Luke."

Luke bowed and left the room. When Luke was out of sight, Lavinia climbed the mahogany staircase. She reached the door to Heath's bedroom. When she was at his door, she hesitated.

Her heart quickened, as she turned the door handle to Heath's bedroom. Heath was lying in his massive bed, his eyes closed. Silk sheets covered him, and Lavinia could clearly see the outline of his maleness. She watched as his breath moved his chest up and down. As far as Lavinia could see, he was still asleep.

She slipped in beside him. She lifted the silk sheet covering him. Her fingers yearned to touch him, her mouth to taste him. Heath began to move, and Lavinia smiled her sultry smile. Heath drew near, and Lavinia expected a kiss. Instead, Heath rolled on top of her, and pinned her arms to the bed. "What are you doing in my bed?" Heath growled out.

Lavinia could feel a hot flush appear on her face. "You didn't appear at dinner."

"And did that bother you?"

"Of course not. I thought you might not be feeling well."

"And coming to my bed is the only way you had of knowing? "Heath didn't wait for an answer from Lavinia. He unpinned her arms, and positioned himself astride her body. As he looked down at her face, he said, "When I want you, Lavinia, you shall know it. When I am ready, you will feel my manhood inside you. I shall come for you, Lavinia."

Lavinia saw the amused expression on Heath's face. She knew he was enjoying her embarrassment. She shoved him off of her. "I shall never surrender to you, Heath. You are attended to by a stable boy, because you mean nothing more to me than a horse in my stable." She got up from the bed, and without a glance back at Heath, she walked out of the room.

When she was out of Heath's view, she fell upon the wall. Huge, heaving sobs poured out of her. She tried to calm herself with deep breaths. When she had calmed down a bit, she walked down the mahogany staircase. She encountered Luke in the hallway. "Are you feeling alright, Marchioness?"

Lavinia did the best she could to compose herself. "I'm fine Luke, thank you. I was just feeling a bit lightheaded. I'm glad you're here. I'll be needing you to get my horse. I'm going for a ride."

"I don't mean to be impertinent, but it's already nighttime. It's too dark to go for a ride."

"You are being impertinent, Luke. I shall do as I please," Lavinia pronounced.

Luke bowed his head. "Very well, Madam. I shall prepare your horse."

Lavinia nodded her head, and watched Luke depart for the stables. She made a determined walk back to her residence. As soon as she reached her bedroom, she rang for her maid. When Dorothy had arrived, she asked her to get her riding outfit. Dorothy hesitated. "Are you sure, Marchioness?"

"Yes, of course. Otherwise, why would I have asked you to bring it to me?"

"Do forgive my impertinence, Madam, but are you sure you want to be riding alone at night? It's not safe."

"I do appreciate your concern, Dorothy, but I feel that a horseback ride is the only way for me to feel any better."

"Very well, Madam." Dorothy brought back a light blue Glengarry riding habit. She assisted her in donning the military style dress, trimmed with lace, braids, and frogs. "Thank you, Dorothy."

"You still need your hat."

"No hat, Dorothy. I want to feel the wind in my hair as I ride. I always liked that feeling."

Dorothy bowed her head. Lavinia took her leave from her room and proceeded to walk to the stable. When she arrived, she found Luke had her horse ready for her. After she mounted the horse, she asked, "Luke, does Heath know I am going for a ride on my horse?"

"Yes, Madam."

"And what was his reaction?"

"He said you are as strong willed as ever, and...."

"Continue," Lavinia encouraged.

"And that it will take more than a horse to break you."

"We shall see about that, Luke." Lavinia prodded her stirrups into the horse and trotted into the riding ring. It was a particularly windy night and Lavinia felt a thrill surge through her as the wind rustled through her hair. She prodded the horse harder and harder until it galloped at a frantic pace.

"Marchioness," she could hear Luke call, "please be careful. The horse looks like it's galloping out of control."

Oblivious to Luke's warnings, Lavinia continued to ride with a wild abandon. Then, she could feel the horse buckle underneath her, and as he kicked up his heels, she was thrown to the ground. "Madam," Luke called as he ran to her. Lavinia lay on the ground, as everything went black around her.

Chapter 11

Luke stood over Lavinia as she lay on the ground. "Madam, can you hear me?"

Lavinia gradually opened her eyes. "I can hear you, Luke>"

"That's good. Can you see me, Madam?"

"Yes, I can see you."

"Good. Now I will go for help to move you. Stay as still as possible, Marchioness."

"Alright. Thank you, Luke."

As Lavinia lay on the ground, she wondered what the extent of her injuries were. She tried to wiggle her fingers, and was glad that she could do that. She wondered if she could move her legs but decided to heed Luke's advice.

She wondered who Luke would get to assist him. She reasoned it would probably be the butler. He seemed like he'd be able to handle the situation. She could hear the sound of footsteps approaching. As she lay on the ground, with increasing pain coursing through her body, she heard the familiar voice. "Lavinia, I'm here to help you."

Lavinia's eyes found Heath's face. "Heath, I'm in pain."

"I know, Lavinia. I am here to rescue you." Lavinia let herself surrender to Heath's authority. He instructed Luke as to how to move Lavinia so there would be a smaller chance of injury. The two men lifted Lavinia off of the ground. Heath carefully placed Lavinia in his arms. Lavinia gazed at Heath as he carried her into the house. Once they entered the house, Heath carried Lavinia up the staircase to her bedroom. He gently dropped her onto the bed. He looked tenderly at her, as he said, "You were very naughty tonight, Marchioness. Can you move your legs?" Lavinia moved her legs and was successful. Heath smiled. "That is good. In all likelihood, there is nothing broken. We shall have to get a doctor here, of course. "

"Of course, Heath. "

Heath sat besides Lavinia on the bed. He ran a finger down her cheek. "You were very naughty tonight, Marchioness. What possessed you to go horseback riding in the evening?"

Lavinia held Heath's gaze for a while. "You, Heath."

"That is very honest, Lavinia. Your honesty pleases me, Lavinia." Lavinia felt an inexplicable thrill at Heath's words. Her private part quivered at his words. She could feel a blush cover her face. Heath's face lowered onto Lavinia's lips and he placed a soft kiss onto her lips.

"Heath, "she said softly, "thank you for rescuing me."

"It is you who rescued me, Lavinia."

"How did I rescue you, Heath?"

"It's so hard to explain, Lavinia. Perhaps I can show you in another way."

Lavinia leaned back against the soft pillows. She was aware of a trembling in her body. Heath slipped in beside her and wrapped his arms around her. She touched his lips with a playful finger. His fingers traced the delicate softness of her lower lip. He gave her lower lip a hungry nibble. Gradually, his mouth moved down her slender throat. Heath's kisses started to arouse a wild need in Lavinia. Lavinia took Heath's palm and pressed a kiss onto it. He kissed her fingertips, and each kiss sent waves of electricity through her veins. His lips settled onto her face, and he kissed her slowly, with a dreamlike intensity.

Lavinia's private parts were growing wet, as Heath's kisses continued. A lusty heat filled her. Lavinia craved him. She placed her hands on his neck, and started to pull him on top of her, but Heath freed himself from her grasp. He got out of the bed and gazed down upon her. She exchanged a puzzled look with him. "Heath, why did you get up?"

"Because, as I told you, I will decide when and if we shall make love."

"Then why did you come to my bed?"

"You need comfort of another sort tonight."

"But..." Lavinia was about to tell Heath how much she craved him, but shame kept her from saying anything.

Heath was well aware of the effect he was having on her. "I told you that I will decide if and when our lovemaking shall begin. I have decided that you aren't up to it tonight, Lavinia. You need your rest. I will send Dorothy to you so she can attend to your needs tonight."

Lavinia almost felt a need to beg Heath to stay with her tonight. However, she fought off the urge, and said briskly, "That will be fine, Heath. Dorothy should be able to attend to my needs tonight."

"Then I will fetch Dorothy now." Heath graced Lavinia with a mock bow and left the room.

Lavinia felt alone as she waited for Dorothy to come to her room. She remembered the nights she had spent with her husband, and they never aroused her they way Heath just did. She wasn't prepared for the torrent of feelings Heath had just released in her.

When the knock on her door came, Lavinia bid Dorothy to enter. She held a tray with a silver teapot and finger sandwiches. "Madam, how are you feeling? I thought you might like something to eat."

"I'm feeling a little sore, but I can move all my body parts."

"I'm so glad, Madam. I did tell you that riding at night wasn't a good idea."

"Yes, you did, Dorothy. Stubborn me should have listened to you, but I've never been known to listen to anyone." Dorothy didn't say anything, but Lavinia said, "It's alright to say what you really feel, Dorothy."

"You are known to be a bit stubborn, Madam, if you forgive my impertinence."

"You're not impertinent, you're speaking the truth."

"Perhaps you can try to be a bit less headstrong, Marchioness."

Lavinia bit into her sandwich and pondered Dorothy's words. She thought of all that had transpired tonight. Her bed felt empty, and all she could think of was how to fill it up again.

CHAPTER 12

When the next morning dawned, Lavinia felt some pain throughout her body. Dorothy had brought her breakfast to her on a silver tray. "How are you feeling this morning, Madam?"

"I'm still sore from the fall, of course. The doctor was kind enough to see me here. He said nothing has been broken, and all he saw were some bruises. He said I was very lucky. "

Lavinia dismissed Dorothy after she had bathed and groomed herself. She helped her to slip into a day dress. Lavinia went back to her bed and drifted off into a light sleep. Visions of last night's encounter with Heath filled her mind. She remembered how safe she felt when he lay beside her. And, she also remembered the ache he had left inside of her, when he decided to leave. She gradually fell into a deeper sleep, and dreamed of Heath

As she lay asleep. She suddenly felt a hand at her shoulder. She looked up to find Heath standing over her. "Is this a dream, or are you really here?"

"Heath Manville is really here, Lavinia." Lavinia tried to control the quiver in her private part. She hoped that her face didn't reveal an embarrassing blush.

"I trust you are feeling a little better than last night."

"A little better. My body still has some pain."

Heath noticed the pitcher of water on Lavinia's desk. He poured water into a glass and then sat down beside her in her bed. He held the glass to her lips. She accepted the water. "You're being very kind this morning, Heath."

"Perhaps I owe you some kindness, Lavinia. After all, if I hadn't rebuffed your offer, you probably wouldn't have engaged in that foolhardy stunt." Lavinia held eye contact with Heath, and for a moment. she felt as if Heath could see into her soul.

"I must say I'm surprised at your kindness, Heath. "

"I suppose you would be. "

"I don't know that much about you, Heath. "

"Are you really interested in knowing more about me, Marchioness?"

Lavinia held eye contact with Heath, and then said, "Yes, I am."

"And what would you like to know about me?"

"What kind of childhood did you have, Heath?"

"A hard one, Lavinia."

"What were your parents like?"

"I grew up with my mother. I was a base born child, and that's the polite way of saying a bastard child."

"I'm sorry, Heath. Did you know who your father was?"

"I did, Lavinia."

"Did your father ever acknowledge you?"

Heath laughed derisively. "His sort would never do that. "

"Heath, who was your father?"

Heath looked away and fell silent. When he looked at Lavinia, he answered, "this isn't the time to tell you, Lavinia."

"Will there ever be a right time, Heath?"

"Perhaps, Lavinia."

"I'm sure it wasn't easy to grow up without a father."

"It wasn't Lavinia. Especially when you know what your life could have been like."

"Then your father must be someone who has some wealth."

'That is enough for now, Lavinia. "Lavinia noted that Heath had a distinctively uncomfortable look on his face. "Lavinia, you can't stay cooped up in here all day. "

"I suppose some fresh air will do me some good. "Heath nodded his approval.

Lavinia slowly rose to a sitting position on the bed. She swung her legs over the edge of the bed and sat still for a while. She tried to get up, but fell back onto the bed. "My body is sorer than I thought." Heath rose from the bed and grabbed her under her arms. He held her steady as her feet landed on the floor. "I can manage on my own, Heath."

"Don't be so obstinate, Lavinia. "

"I'm not being obstinate, it's just that I'm used to walking on my own."

"I'm paying off my debt to you, Lavinia. Please let me."

"There really is no debt to pay off. Last night was just a moment of madness."

"Rest your head on my shoulder, Lavinia." Lavinia obeyed Heath's request. "Shall I call Dorothy to help you put on your shoes?"

"Yes, I think that would be a good idea." Heath rang for Dorothy, and then placed Lavinia in a chair. "After you get your shoes on, we will take a stroll in the gardens."

Heath waited for Lavinia in the hallway. When Dorothy had finished, he entered Lavinia's bedroom. "We are ready for our walk, Lavinia." Heath held Lavinia under the arms as he assisted her down the staircase.

When they reached the hallway, Lavinia said, "Thank you, Heath, but I think I am strong enough to walk on my own."

"I am glad to hear that, Lavinia. I am always here to assist you."

They walked out into the warm, spring day. "Heath, have you ever seen my garden?"

"No, I haven't. but I would enjoy that."

Lavinia smiled as they walked along a path sprinkled with elm trees. Sunny daffodils joined blue bells in the surrounding woodlands. They reached the center of the garden. A fountain stood at the center of the garden. Lavinia pointed to a bench underneath a tree. "This is a nice place to sit, Heath."

Heath joined Lavinia on the bench. "Your garden is beautiful, Lavinia."

Lavinia nodded. "I come here to just be still and enjoy the nature."

"It is peaceful here, Lavinia."

Lavinia looked curiously at Heath. "I never thought of you as a man who would seek peace."

"I'm not an animal, Lavinia.'

"I didn't mean to imply that you were, Heath."

"Didn't you once imply I was like a horse?"

"Perhaps I was a bit harsh. I've had a chance to get to know you more. You shared something about your childhood with me."

Heath held Lavinia's hand. "I've gotten a chance to know you more, too, Lavinia."

Encouraged by the warm gesture, Lavinia felt she could ask something more. "Heath, you told me something about your childhood. How did your mother support you?"

"She was a scullery maid most of the time. Sometimes..." Heath hesitated.

"You don't have to tell me, Heath."

"Sometimes she was forced to be a lady bird." Heath watched Lavinia's reaction. "I hope I haven't offended you. Not every-one is lucky enough to be a Marchioness. Some women are forced to sell their bodies out of desperation."

"I don't judge your mother, Heath. I, myself, have been judged. My husband's parents think I am a jade."

"I suppose they would be afraid that a woman of loose morals would mar the reputation of their late son being that they are titled members of the aristocracy."

"You seem so bitter, Heath. What has made you so bitter towards the aristocracy?'

"When you are brought up in privilege, it's hard to under-stand how those less fortunate feels."

"You are wrong, Heath. I understand more than you know. I have never felt at home in the aristocracy. People have always wanted me to be something that I wasn't."

"I know you long to be who you truly are. I can help you, Lavinia. "

"You can, Heath?"

"I can free you."

"Free me from what?"

"I think you know, Lavinia. I can be the man you have always desired. "Heath pulled Lavinia close to him and claimed her lips. He wrapped his arms around her waist and scooped her up in his arms. He showered kisses upon her face as he carried her back to the house.

CHAPTER 13

"Heath, why are you carrying me? I'm perfectly capable of walking."

"Isn't this more exciting, Lavinia?"

"I don't want the servants to think I'm not able to walk on my own power."

Heath disregarded Lavinia's protests and carried her to her home. Dorothy saw them when they entered the hallway. She quickly put her head down, and remained quiet as Heath carried Lavinia up the staircase.

Heath gently dropped Lavinia down on to the bed. "Heath, Dorothy saw you carry me up the staircase. What will she think?"

"Lavinia, this isn't the time to worry about what the servants will think. You never put much store in what the ton thinks. Why bother with the servants?"

"Servants can have loose tongues, and I don't want them spreading rumors about me to fellow servants. Gossip spreads quickly, and I am trying to get my rightful inheritance."

"Lavinia, I told you that if we ever make love, it will be when I decide to." Lavinia lay quietly on the bed, as a lusty feeling of warmth swept over her. Heath undid the stays on her dress, and slipped it off of her. Lavinia could see Heath's eyes caress her as his eyes traveled down her body. Her fingers yearned to touch him, and her mouth to taste him. "Now is the time, Lavinia. "

Heath lay beside Lavinia on the bed. His fingers traced the delicate softness of her lower lip. He cupped her head and kissed her lips. His mouth was on hers, bestowing tender kisses onto her. Her lips were warm and welcoming. Then Heath broke the kiss and bit her lower lip. He gave her lower lip a hungry nibble. His mouth moved down her slender throat. Heath's kisses aroused a sharp need that had been buried in Lavinia for so long. She returned Heath's kisses with a wild passion. She ravaged his mouth with kisses. He pulled her close, kissing the nape of her neck. Heath's kisses crashed into her heart.

Heath nuzzled the inside of her thigh. His hand reached for that most womanly and secret part of her. His fingers stroked her, as Lavinia was sent into shivers of ecstasy. She writhed against his hand, lost to pleasure. Lavinia was eager to give Heath pleasure. She wrapped one slender hand around his growing manhood. She could feel him grow even harder in her hands. She made a fist around his shaft and began to move it back and forth. "Lavinia, I am going to find out what secrets are hiding inside that soft flesh."

Lavinia was powerless to resist Heath's raw masculinity. Every inch of her lit up with the burning, urgent need to possess him. He parted her thighs, as Lavinia's opening throbbed for him. She was wet and ready, as his erection slid across the damp curls between her legs. He pushed his heavy erection against her opening. He moved himself inside of her, and as his erection filled her, they moved together as one. He pressed harder into her, deeper, filling her up with his maleness. Arching her hips, she met him thrust for thrust. She moved under him, moaning as he filled her. She locked her legs around him, holding him captive to her lust. Her whole body was on fire with pleasure as Heath's rough thrusts continued. Then, as he reached his climax, he filled his seed into her. Lavinia's body gave a surprised jerk, and then melted into his. Heath lay on top of her, and Lavinia looked into Heath's whiskey eyes. The eyes she had seen in the carriage that night.

Lavinia lay in Heath's arms. She had never experienced a connection like this with her husband. They lay quietly, wrapped together in the blissful afterglow. Lavinia settled into Heath's embrace. Heath kissed Lavinia's forehead. "I have made you mine. You know that, don't you, Lavinia?"

"I don't know that, Heath.

"You are most stubborn lady, Lavinia."

Lavinia didn't answer immediately. "Heath, I didn't want this to happen."

"I think that you did, Lavinia. I think this is what you wanted ever since you first saw me in that carriage."

"Heath, I didn't want to ever be controlled by a man again. I didn't want a man to ever have that kind of power over me again."

"Your husband had a different kind of power over you, Lavinia. He had the power of status and wealth, and everything society could offer you. I, on the other hand, can give you what you have always craved." Heath kissed her mouth, and it crashed into her heart.

"We still have that matter of training you to be a proper Marquis."

"I will be a proper Marquis to you, Lavinia. In ever way that matters." Heath rolled over Lavinia's body and entered her again. Lavinia knew that Heath had made her his woman.

CHAPTER 14

One week later

"Have I made any progress, Marchioness?" Heath attempted a very graceful bite of his roll.

"I do see some improvement but we still have some work to do before you are acceptable to my late husband's parents."

"Have you seen any improvement in other areas, Marchioness?"

"There can always be improvements made."

Heath stood over Lavinia and kissed her neck. "And do you enjoy the practice sessions, Marchioness?"

Lavinia slapped Heath's hand. "Ssh, there are servants walking around. We don't want them to get the wrong idea."

"I thought other people's opinions didn't matter that much to you, Marchioness."

"It does when vast amounts of money and property are involved."

Heath sat down on the adjacent chair. "Marchioness, we're going to take a trip today."

"We don't have time for a vacation, Heath. We have a lot of work to do before you are fully trained."

Heath got up. He scooped Lavinia out of the chair. "What are you doing? Put me down at once."

Heath didn't answer. He held her in his strong arms until they reached the stables. He attached the horses to the gig. He lifted Lavinia into the gig. He took the reins of the horse and they started their journey.

"Heath, I demand that you tell me where we are going."

"We are going to my childhood home."

"But why, Heath? I should think that you would want to forget that part of your life."

"But I can't forget that part of my life, Lavinia. It will always be a part of me. "

"But why now? When we are so close to inheriting all my late husband's money?"

"You can train me to be a proper Marquess, but you can't destroy the part of me that makes me a man."

"I don't wish to destroy you as a man, Heath."

"We shall see, my dear Marchioness."

The hours passed and soon they were in the middle of a village. "we're on Great Earl Street," Lavinia noted. "Heath, we're in the Seven Dials."

"That's right, my dear. You're in the poor part of town."

"Whatever for?"

"Because this is where I grew up, Marchioness. Not everyone lived like the high born."

"You sound so bitter, Heath."

"I grew up in poverty, Lavinia. Sometimes a hard upbringing can do that to you."

"So why come back to a place filled with bitter memories?"

Heath pulled up outside a house. "This is why, Lavinia. This is where my mother lives."

"And why have you brought me here?"

"Isn't it customary for a future wife to meet her future husband's family?"

"Yes, of course."

"This is my family, Lavinia."

"I shall be honored to meet your mother, Heath."

Heath helped Lavinia out of the gig and they walked to the door of the house. They pulled the rope and waited. A pretty blonde woman opened the door. "Heath, you've come home. Your mother has been asking for you. Please come in."

Heath and Lavinia entered. "I'm surprised to see you here, Arabella."

"I've been helping your mother."

"Is she ill?" Arabella fell silent. "She is ill." Heath studied the woman's expression. "She's dying, isn't she?"

"I'm afraid so, Heath."

"Where is she?"

"In her bedroom."

Lavinia followed Heath into the bedroom. Heath's mother looked frail in the bed, but she managed a smiled when she saw her son. She extended her arms to him. "Heath, I willed you here."

"I shouldn't have stayed away for so long, Mother."

"A man has to find his own way in life."

"And that can be very hard for a man to do."

"Have you found your way, son?"

"I'm not sure, Mother. I have found a wife, though. I'd like to introduce you to my future wife, the Marchioness of Coltfield."

Heath's mother looked Lavinia down from head to toe. "Oh, aren't we fancy? So, the lady is a Marchioness. And how could you lower yourself to come to my humble abode?"

"Mother, Lavinia is a different sort of Marchioness. She doesn't put much store in the ways of the ton."

"Don't you believe that, son. She's just like all the other members of the so-called haute monde. All that nonsense about titles and blood lines. She's just as evil as all the others of her ilk."

"You do sound bitter," Lavinia said.

"I have reason to, my dear LadyLavinia. Did you know you're about to marry the son of a duke? And the first born one, I might add."

Lavinia exchanged looks with Heath. "Is this true?"

Heath nodded. "It is, Lavinia. I am the side slip of the Duke of Manchester."

"Heath, I know the Duke. He was a good friend of my late husband. He has two daughters. He never had a son. Did he ever acknowledge you?"

"He gave me a sum of money when Heath was born, but I never heard from him again. I wasn't high born enough for him to marry. Instead, he married the daughter of an Earl."

"I've heard his marriage is very unhappy. He's known to frequent Gentlemen's clubs quite frequently."

"He'll never change, that one. The only thing he gave Heath was childhood of struggle. I made a miserable living as a seamstress. "

"I'm so sorry, "Lavinia offered.

"Do you know what would make me a happy woman before I die? I would like to know that Heath will inherit his rightful share of the Duke's money, or at least be offered some kind of settlement."

"And how can I make that happen?," Heath wondered.

"Life can be strange, Heath. Fate has brought you to the Marchioness. Perhaps she could give you entry into the Duke's world. You mentioned that you knew him."

Heath looked at Lavinia . He saw she was about to say something, but he cut in. "Lavinia shall be glad to arrange an introduction for me."

"I'd like to hear that from her, son. Will you do that for my son, Lavinia. I have a present from him that is inscribed with my name. "

Lavinia saw the tears swimming in her eyes. She saw the imploring look in Heath's eyes. "I will."

She extended her hand for Lavinia to take. "Then you have my blessings for this marriage, Marchioness. If you do this, I will know that you truly love my son."

Lavinia took her hand. "I do love your son, with my whole heart and soul."

"I know I will live long enough to be at your wedding. "

Heath took his mother's other hand. "I know you will be at our wedding, Mother." Heath and Lavinia gazed into each other's eyes, both happy that they pleased Heath's mother.

CHAPTER 15

After the journey back to the country estate, Heath and Lavinia enjoyed their dinner. "Lavinia," Heath began, "I asked you to think about something as we traveled back to the countryside."

"You asked me to think about whether I would introduce you to the Duke."

"Have you thought about it?"

" I have."

"Your answer, Marchioness."

Lavinia drew a deep breath. "Heath, I don't think I can do what you asked."

" So what you told my mother about helping me was all a lie."

"Don't put it that way, Heath. I was trying to give a dying woman some peace."

"But you don't really care about her son, do you?"

Lavinia touched Heath's arm. "But I do, Heath. I care about you with my whole heart and soul."

"But you care more about your possessions and about your position in society."

"That's important to me as well, of course."

"Of course? Then you are no different than the other members of you're the so called high born."

"But I am different, Heath. You must believe me."

"How can I believe you, Marchioness, when you have refused to honor my request?'

"Heath, you must understand. My husband's parents would never allow you into the family. There would be a scandal, and it could ruin the chances of any relatives to marry well."

Heath stood up. "Then you have chosen, Marchioness. You have chosen your position in society over my love for you."

"I love you also, Heath." She stood face to face with Heath. "But I would lose everything."

"There's also a chance that I could gain the Duke's inheritance."

"Heath, that would never happen. The Duke has a family and reputation to think about. "

Heath fixed Lavinia with such an angry gaze that she could almost feel her insides shrivel up. He abruptly turned his back on her and started to walk away. "Heath, where are you going? What will you do? "

He halted and turned to look at Lavinia with a sad smile. Although Heath didn't answer, Lavinia got a sinking feeling in her stomach as she watched him walk out of the diningroom.

She sank back into her chair , as tears began to sting her eyes. She knew in her heart that Heath wouldn't be coming to her bedroom tonight. And it wasn't only the physical passion that she would miss. She would miss the strong arms wrapped around her, that made her feel so safe. She only hoped that her worse fears wouldn't come true.

CHAPTER 16

Lavinia ate her breakfast alone for the first time in two weeks.. She waited for Heath's arrival as she bit into her roll. Her breakfast had no appeal to her this morning .There wasn't any Heath to chide into being a proper Marquess. She felt his absence keenly as she sat in her empty diningroom. She decided to see where Heath was.

A heavy sense of foreboding weighed Lavinia down as she walked to Heath's cottage. Nerves fluttered in her belly as she waited for the door to open, afraid her worse fear had come true. "Good morning ,Marchioness," Luke said.

She entered the hallway. " I've come to see Sir Heath."

"He isn't here Marchioness."

Her breath caught in her throat. "Do you know where he went?"

"He left this morning in the gig. He left you this letter."

Lavinia sat on the setee as Luke went to get the letter. She felt faint as she braced herself for what she would read in Heath's letter. Luke handed Lavinia the letter. Her hands shook as she opened the envelope and read what Heath had written.

Dear Lavinia,

It is with mixed feelings that I write this letter to you. Last night, I asked you to make a choice. And you chose the trappings of society over love. I understand why you made that choice, but it's a choice I can't accept.

Lavinia, I love you and it is incredibly difficult for me to leave you. But I can't give up the part of me that wants to right the wrong that had been done to my mother, And make no mistake, I will right it, with or without your help.

Goodbye, my dear Lavinia. I do wish only happiness for you.

Lavinia tried to gulp back the tears which slid down her cheeks. She peeked a look at Luke , who tried to stand without expression. "Luke, I know this is unladylike, but I need some brandy."

"Of course, Marchioness."

"And bring an extra glass."

Luke brought back a tray with a bottle of brandy and two glasses. "Luke, please sit down and have a drink with me."

"That is highly unusual, Marchioness."

"I know, Luke, but I'm so tired of all the rules that we all have to follow. Please sit down and have a drink with me."Luke poured the drinks and then sat opposite Lavinia. "Luke, did Heath tell you where he was going?"

"No, Marchioness." Luke looked kindly at his employer. "Marchioness, do I have your permission to be frank?"

"You do, Luke."

" Go after him."

"What?"

"Find him, Marchioness."

"But where would I look?"

" Where do you think Heath would be most comfortable?"

"I should think he would want to be with people who understand him."

"I do too. Perhaps he has a favorite part of town?"

Lavinia put down her drink. "You've known all along, haven't you, Luke?"

" I've known that Heath really wasn't Sir Heath. He just didn't have the manners of the upper class."

" It's time we all stop pretending. It's time for the truth. And the truth is that I love Heath . "

"Then you must go after him. Don't let your happiness slip away from you, Marchioness."

"But he doesn't wish to have anything to do with me."

" Marchioness, I've seen the way Heath's face lit up when he spoke about you. He might not have shown it, but he lived for the moments he could be with you. Men don't always show their feelings as easily as women. Especially men who have grown up in rougher conditions."

" I do have a sense that he is in the Seven Dials."

"Don't worry, Madam. I will gp with you and be your protector."

"That's very kind, Luke. " Lavina took another sip of her drink. "Please prepare my coach. I am going to find the man I love."

Chapter 17

Lavinia watched the hillside roll past her as she sat in her carriage. The serenity of nature had an almost soothing effect on her, and she might have been contented to enjoy it, if it weren't for one fact. She had lost the man she loved, and didn't even know where he was. And ,as she dwelled on her vow to get him back, the carriage suddenly halted.

"Now's not the time for one of the horses to fall prey to an injury. Please let it be something else, " she pleaded to the top of her carriage. Lavinia peered out of her carriage window, to see a man on a dark horse, holding one gun pointed at Luke, and another gun pointed at the carriage. "But not that."

She took a deep breath and then opened the carriage door. "What is the meaning of this?"

" Stand and deliver," the man on the horse commanded.

"Marchioness, do what the man says. He's a highwayman."

"So I've selected a Marchioness. Get out of the carriage."

As the horror of her situation gripped her, Lavinia clutched the reticule she carried with her. She held the reticule to her bosom, and just as her legs touched the ground, she took her pistol out of the reticule. She pointed the pistol at the robber and pierced his shoulder with a bullet. The horse whinnied and threw up his front legs. As he aimlessly pulled the trigger of his gun, Lavinia was herded into the coach by Luke. "We should be in Seven Dials shortly."

Lavinia looked at the robber as the coach pulled away. He was holding his shoulder, and was clearly struggling to get up. She didn't know what would happen to him, and she didn't care. All she knew was that he had almost gotten in the way of finding Heath. And that had given Lavinia the strength to use her pistol against him. Lavinia's hand started to hurt. And when she looked at it, she noticed that it was red and swollen. Lavinia endured a bumpy ride along the road leading to the Seven Dials. "Heath, " she said to herself, "if only you knew what I had to endure for you."

At last, the towers of the Seven Dials loomed before her. She had given Luke the address of Heath's mother before they left. As she saw the house loom into view, her stomach clenched. If Heath was in the house, she would have to convince him that she truly loved him, or else risk losing him forever.

Luke opened the carriage door for her. As he helped her down from the carriage, je noticed her swollen hand. "Madam, that hand needs attention. "

"Later, Luke. "

"As you wish, Madam." Luke walked with Lavinia to the door.

When the door opened, Lavinia recognized the pretty blonde woman who was attending Heath's mother. "Ow, it's you," the Cockney voice said. "You've done enough. What do you want with Heath now?"

"Please , is he here?"

"Aven't you done enough? "

"How do you know what I've done?"

She hesitated, and then said, "It doesn't take much to figure out what the likes of your kind can do. "

"Please, if he isn't here, can you tell me where he is?"

"It's alright. " Lavinia recognized the deep timbre of Heath's voice. He stood in the hallway, and gave a mock bow. " Enter, Marchioness."

Lavinia and Luke entered the hallway. "Heath, I'm so glad I've found you."

" And why is that, Marchioness? "

"Sir," Luke said. "The Marchioness has been through a lot. "

Heath scanned Lavinia with a derisive look that bore through her soul. Her hand grasped her heart. When Heath saw her hand, his voice was firm. "Marchioness, let me see your hand."

"My hand is fine, Heath."

"No, it's not." He gently pulled her hand away from her chest. "That looks like a bullet graze. What has happened to you?"

" We were accosted by a highwayman. The Marchioness showed true bravery, She shot him with her pistol."

" Silly fool," Heath scolded. "Your money and jewels weren't worth your life, and Luke's life."

" Sir, don't you see? The Marchioness loves you so much that she risked her life so she could see you again."

Heath sought out Lavinia's eyes. "Marchioness, is this true?"

"Yes, Heath it's true. I love you, and I don't care who knows it. I'll do anything you ask, just as long as I can be with you."

"Don't be fooled by those words, Heath," Annabelle said. "You can't trust the ilk of her."

" I didn't raise a fool." Heath turned to see his mother standing in the hallway.

" Mother, you should be resting."

"I've still got some life left in me, Heath. If this woman risked her life to see you, then she is the woman for you. "

Heath got down on one knee. "Marchioness, can I have the honor of being your husband?"

"Yes, Heath."

Heath rose to face Lavinia. "But first we have to get that hand to a doctor."

" Just tell me where to go, Sir."

"Wait," Lavinia said. "Before we go, I want to invite your mother to our wedding. It will take place next month."

"No matter what?" Heath inquired.

"No matter what." Heath put his arm around Lavinia's shoulder and led her to the coach.

TRANSFERENCE

No matter what, Heath put his arms up Lavinia's hand and held her to the truth.

Chapter 18

Heath gently kissed Lavinia's face as they lay together in the bedroom of her London townhouse. "Let me look at your hand." Lavinia let Heath examine her hand. "The doctor did a good job. Your hand will be as good as new. But if I ever hear of you doing anything that silly again,I'll..."

"You'll what?"

"Never mind. There won't be any need. I'll always be here to protect you."

"Heath, 29 days have passed since you've been here. Tomorrow night we will hold our party. My husband's parents will be there to meet you. "

"And, if all goes according to plan, so will the Duke of Manchester."

" Are you prepared for what can happen?"

"I am prepared, Lavinia. Either the Duke will openly acknowledge me as his son, or I will probably punch him in his face."

"Heath, the chances of the Duke acknowledging you is very small. And if you punch him in the nose, you will end up in goal again .I will certainly need my inheritance to keep you out of goal."

" Yes, you are right, Marchioness. I will have to mind my manners tomorrow night."

"Heath , what will you do if the Duke does acknowledge you?"

"Then I will demand what is rightfully mine. " Heath propped himself up on his elbow and looked down at Lavinia. "Are you prepared for what could happen?"

"Heath, I know what will happen. My husband's parents will never stand for the scandal this will cause. So, either I lose my inheritance, and the Duke doesn't acknowledge you, and we are forced to struggle on our own, or the Duke does acknowledge you and you get your fair share of his estate."

"And you are prepared to lose your position in society?"

Lavinia laughed. "My position in society? I'm already known as a bit of a trollop. In fact, I think I should rather enjoy seeing the looks on all the aristocrats who will be there."

"It's easier to speak about what will happen, than to actually be prepared for the consequences."

"Heath, how can I convince you that I am truly ready for what will happen?"

"There is one way. I will know it when I make love to you tonight, Lavinia. I will see it on your face, and sense it in your heart and soul. "

"I hope I will be satisfactory to you tonight, Sir Heath."

"Then no more talk. Let us proceed." He clenched his fingers into her hair. His fingers traced the delicate softness of her lower lip with his other hand. His mouth found hers, and he took her lips with his own. His kiss was hard, then soft, then hard again. She retuned his kiss with a wild passion. Both their souls were on fire, as his hand reached for that most womanly and secret part of her. His fingers stroked her, sending her into shivers of ecstacy.

Lavinia was eager to return the pleasure Heath gave her. She wrapped one slender hand around the hard flesh of his shaft. She slid her hand up and down the length of him. She could feel his growing arousal, and she knew he was hard for her, and only her. Heath parted her thighs, as her opening throbbed for him. His erection slid across the damp curls between her legs.He moved himself against her, and they moved together as one. He pushed himself into the heated core of her body. He thrust into her, as she rotated her hips in slow circles around his organ. He pressed harder into her, deeper, filling her up with his maleness. She moved under him, moaning as he filled her. Powerful sensations built inside of Lavinia. She grabbed his hair and pulled him close. The growing heat she felt increased until she found release with a soul shattering climax. They both lay still in mutual surrender.

Lavinia lay with him, relishing their connection. "Have I convinced you, Heath?"

Heath touched her lips with a playful finger. "Yes, my darling Lavinia, you have convinced me. Tomorrow night I will have my meeting with the Duke and it will be arranged by you. And no matter what happens, you will be my future wife."

" No matter what," Lavinia agreed. Their lips met and kissed away any doubt or fear.

CHAPTER 19

Lavinia and Heath stood at the entrance of the door to the ballroom. Lavinia looked at the sea of guests dressed in beautiful gowns and adorned with jewels. She looked into Heath's eyes. "Are you ready, Heath?"

"Yes, I am. Are you ready, Lavinia? Are you prepared for whatever may happen?"

" Yes, Heath, I am." She squeezed Heath's hand, smiled, and they walked together into the ballroom.

Lavinia admired the décor of the ballroom as they entered. She wanted to be certain that everything would be perfect for this evening's events. She was pleased at the flickering candles which adorned the tables. Flowers adorned the numerous tables, at which the esteemed members of the ton sat. Musicians were posted in the balcony, and played the strains to a country dance.

Heath faced Lavinia and graced her with a slight bow. " May I have the honor of this dance, Marchioness?"

" I don't know if you're on my dance card, but I think you will do, Sir Heath."

Lavinia and Heath took their place at the head of the line. She knew that there would be people looking at the dancers on the floor. This was the moment she had trained Heath for. He was standing in front of the ladies and gentlemen of the ton, and their eyes were upon him. The musicians played the strains of a country dance, and Lavinia and Heath made their way down the line. Lavinia noticed the stares which the ladies cast his way. Lady Howlington approached them after the dance was over. " Lady Coltfield, you must introduce me to your dance partner."

"This is Sir Heath. He's my future husband."

" Why Lavinia, you've caught a Prince."

" Not a Prince, Lady Howlington. Just a man who is in love with a Princess," Heath said with a slight bow.

"And to think you've fallen in love with a...."

"A what, Lady Howlington?" Lavinia prodded.

" Never mind."

"No, please speak your truth."

" The last time I saw you , you were sprawled out on the ground with a stable boy on top of you."

"Is the word you're looking for a trollop, perhaps?"

" Lavinia, I'll never understand you. "

" I suppose not, Lady Howlington."

"Lady Howlington," Heath said, "I'd be delighted if you'd join us at our table. "

" Thank you, Sir Heath. "

"Please allow me the pleasure of escorting you to our table."

Heath led Lady Howlington to one of several tables which were set up in the ballroom. The men at the table rose when Lavinia and Lady Howlington sat down.

"The white soup is delicious," the dowager Lady Coltfield pronounced.

"Best I've ever tasted," Lord Coltfield said.

Lavinia smiled as she watched Heath sip his soup in silence. She remembered the time she heard him sip his soup in her diningroom. He had come so far.

Heath sat to Lavinia's right. " We certainly have some esteemed guests at our table. Lord and Lady Howlington, Lord and Lady Coltfield, and the Duke and Duchess of Manchester." Heath saw the Duke glance his way .He wondered if had occurred to him that he shared the same hair color, same, eyes, and same cheekbone structure that he had.

Lavinia thought that Heath was the spitting image of the Duke. She noticed that the Duke cast a few glances towards Heath. If she had ever doubted that he was really the Duke's son, this remarkable resemblance convinced her that Heath truly was the Duke's sideslip.

When the mutton arrived at the table, Lavinia pronounced, " Sir Heath will carve the meat tonight, because he is my intended husband." Lavinia saw the immediate stares which Lord and Lady Coltfield cast towards Heath.

"Did I pass inspection,Lord Coltfield? "

"I wouldn't put it that way," he answered. "After all, you're not a show horse."

The Duke of Manchester laughed heartily. " You have good humour, Sir Heath. I'm afraid he's quite right, Lord Coltfield. The members of the ton do take ourselves entirely too seriously."

Heath turned his attention to Lord Manchester. "I assume you are enjoying the evening, Duke Manchester."

"Yes, of course. The food is very tasty, and the ladies are certainly beautiful."

"You always have had an eye for the ladies."

The Duke looked aghast, but chuckled. "England has produced it's fair share of English roses. I just have my share of national pride." He looked appreciatively at his wife.

" Yes, you have appreciated many a beauty in your life," Heath agreed.

"See here, Sir Heath, what is the meaning of this line of conversation?" the Duke demanded.

"Your Grace, your appreciation of our English roses has produced a bastard child. And you are looking at him."

"That is preposterous. I have only produced children with my wife."

Lord Coltfield quickly interjected. "Lavinia, what madness does this man speak? How can he be so uncouth as to speak about this at a dinner party? And this is the man you hope will get our approval?"

The Duke fixed his eyes on Heath. "See here. This is nonsense. Anyone can say that he is the son of a Duke, and would have good reason to do so. But can you prove it?"

Heath took the locket out of his pocket. He rose and handed it to the Duke. The Duke held it in his hand and looked at ithe back of the locket. "The inscription bears my coat of arms. Where did you steal this from?"

"It's not stolen, your Grace. I saw Heath's mother hand it to him as she lay on her sick bed."

" Fiona is sick?" The Duke knew he had made a mistake as soon as the words left his mouth.

"Henry, do you know this woman? ", his wife inquired.

The Duke was about to utter something, but then fell silent. He stared at his wife who had horror etched into her face. "Arabella, I can't lie anymore. " He touched his wife's arm. "I'm afraid I have some bad news to share. Bad news I received from my doctor."

"Henry, what is it?"

" My heart is weak, Arabella. I don't know how much longer I will be here. " The Duke saw his wife sobbing but continued on. " We have produced no sons, and I was always worried about you being alone after I am gone." The Duke rose and faced Heath. " This man is speaking the truth. You are my son, Heath."

"Lavinia, did you know that Heath was going to expose himself as a bastard child?" Lord Coltfield demanded.

" I knew he was going to expose himself as the rightful son of the Duke of Manchester. Bastard is the word society uses, but it is not how I see him."

" Of course you don't, Lavinia. You have always tried to set up one's bristles." Lady Coltfield said. "But you have gone too far this time. Sir Heath, or whoever he is, can never get our approval as your husband. So either you give up this marriage, or you are disinherited."

Heath held Lavinia's eyes , He waited silently for her reply. "Then disinheritance it will be, Lady Coltfield."

" I told my son to never marry you. You were an embarrassment to our family from the start. I want it to be clear to everyone that Lady Coltfield and I are entirely divorced from you. "

"But I am not," the Duke pronounced. "I don't know how much longer I have to live. And it's made me see how petty the so called haute monde can be. We all go to church on Sunday, like good Christians, but we fall far short of following Christian values. " The Duke faced Heath. " I have fallen far short of my responsibilities to you. I welcome you into my family, son." He extended his hand for Heath to shake.

Heath accepted his hand. The Duke extended his arm, in a welcoming gesture to Lavinia. She smiled and moved into the circle that they formed. Lavinia knew that she had made the right choice. She had followed the choice of her heart.

CHAPTER 20

Lavinia stood outside the porticos of St. Georges church. She wanted to be sure everything was perfect for her wedding day. The Duke had sent her to the most fashionable dressmaker in London to design her wedding gown. She admired the fine white muslin gown embroidered with primroses . She luxuriated in the white silk shawl embossed with white satin flowers on her shoulder. "Elizabeth, does my bonnet look good?"

" You look beautiful, Marchioness." Elizabeth handed her a small bouquet of flowers.

"Thank you for attending to me on my wedding day."

" Just think, when I see you again you will be the Duchess of Manchester."

Lavinia smiled, and walked through the church door Elizabeth had opened for her.

The Duke of Manchester was waiting for her at the door. He smiled and she crooked her arm through him as they walked down the aisle. Lavinia saw Heath standing at the front of the church. She felt like her chest was going to explode with emotion when she saw Heath dressed in his embroidered waistcoat. When she had reached the front of the church, Lavinia's eyes sought her groom's eyes. As they held eye contact, she knew there wasn't any need for words. The love shining in his eyes touched the deepest part of her heart.

The Vicar proceeded with the ceremony. At last, the ring was blessed and Heath placed the ring on Lavinia's finger. Lavinia' heart couldn't keep still as she heard Heath declare, "with this ring I thee wed, with my body I thee worship, and with all my wordly goods I thee endow. In the Name of the Father, and of the Son, and of the Holy Ghost. Amen."

Lavinia and Heath started their walk out of the church. The guests followed behind them and the wedding procession had begun. Lavinia smiled at the children in the street who were showering seeds and rice on them.

Lavinia and Heath had reached the Duke's coach which would take them to his estate for their wedding breakfast. The Duke said, " You and your bride can take my coach to my estate. I will ride with your mother, Heath, and we will meet you at my home."

" I'm so glad you were well enough to see us married," Lavinia said.

" When I heard Heath was marrying the woman he loved, it gave me the strength to get up from my bed. "

"I told your mother she will have nothing but the best medical care from now on."

"Duke, you must be careful, or you'll change my viewpoint about the haute monde."

"That's exactly what I intend to do."

" I dare say my mother has suffered enough. I'm glad you have found peace, Mother."

" I have, Heath. Nothing could give me more peace than to know you will spend your life with the woman you love."

" Then you will have your peace, Mother, because I love the Duchess of Manchester with my whole heart and soul."

Lavinia touched Heath's face. " I have given you my heart on this day, and forever."

Heath scooped Lavinia up into his arms and deposited her in the coach. He took his place beside her on the seat and held her hand, as they journeyed to the wedding breakfast which would launch them into their new life as husband and wife.

EPILOGUE

1 year later

Lavinia and Heath walked through the great hall of the Duke of Manchester's estate. "Heath, your father collected the most amazing statues."" I agree. He had a fondness for Italian statues. " They continued their walk to the drawing room. They sat down on the setee. "Life can take many strange twists and turns, Heath."" You are right, Lavinia. When I was sitting in goal, I'd never have thought the Dule of Manchester would have left me one of his estates. And...." Heath stopped and pulled Lavinia in closer to him. "I'd never have thought that I'd be married to a woman as beautiful as you are, Lavinia."" I never thought that I'd be allowed to find happiness with.. " Lavinia stopped herself."Continue, Lavinia.""With a man who punched a Duke."" Have you found happiness, Lavinia?"She placed a tender kiss on Heath's cheek. " I will show you how happy you have made me." She took Heath's hand and placed it on her stomach. He glanced up at Lavinia's radiant face. " Lavinia, you are going to have our baby."" Yes, I am, Heath.""Then my happiness is complete, Lavinia. " He ran his finger down her cheek, and kissed her tenderly. He pulled away, and asked, "Is your happiness complete, Lavinia?"Lavinia took her husband's hand. "More than I could have ever dreamed was possible for me in this world that we live in, Heath." He pulled her into him, wrapped his arms around her waist, and Lavinia knew she had found the man she would love for the rest of her life.

Ingram Content Group UK Ltd.
Milton Keynes UK
UKHW020640050623
422889UK00016B/1958

9 780932 163127